# Contents

# Enid Blyton

# HAPPY CHRISTMAS, FIVE

illustrated by **Jamie Littler**

*h*

Hodder
Children's
Books

A division of Hachette Children's Books

# Famous Five Colour Reads

For a complete list of the full-length
Famous Five adventures, turn to
the last page of this book

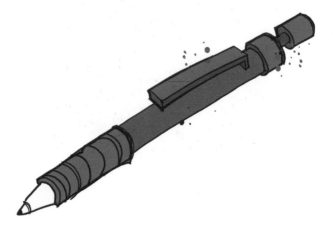

# CHAPTER ONE

**Christmas Eve** at Kirrin Cottage – and **the Five** were all there **together!** They were up in the boys' bedroom, wrapping Christmas presents in bright paper. Timmy was very excited, and nosed about the room, his long tail wagging in delight.

'Don't keep slapping my legs with your tail, Tim,' said Anne. **'Look out,** George, he's getting tangled up with your ball of string!'

7

'Don't look round, Anne, I'm wrapping up your present,' said Dick. 'There'll be a lot to give out this Christmas, with all of us here – and everyone giving everyone else something!'

'I've a B-O-N-E for Timmy,' said Anne, 'but it's downstairs in the larder. I was afraid he'd **sniff it out** up here.'

**'Woof,'** said Timmy, slapping his tail against Anne's legs again.

'He knows perfectly well that B-O-N-E spells **bone,**' said Julian. 'Now you've made him **sniff** all about **my parcels!** Timmy – go downstairs, **please!**'

'Oh no – he does so love Christmas time, and helping us to wrap up parcels,' said George. **'Sit, Timmy. SIT**, I say. That's the third time you've knocked down my pile of presents.'

Downstairs, her father and mother were wrapping up parcels, too. They seemed to have as many as the **four cousins** upstairs! Mrs Kirrin looked at the pile of packages on the table.

'Far too many to go on the **tree!**' she said. 'We'd better put **all our parcels** and the **children's too** into **a sack**, Quentin. We can stand the sack at the bottom of the tree, and **you** can be **Father Christmas** and hand them out tomorrow morning.'

'I am **NOT** going to be **Father Christmas,'** said Mr Kirrin. 'All this **nonsense** at **Christmas time!** Bits of paper everywhere – parcels to undo – **Timmy barking** his head off. **Listen to him now! I'll go mad!** He's to go to his kennel.'

'No, no, Quentin – don't upset George on Christmas Eve,' said Mrs Kirrin. 'Look – you go and sit down quietly in your study and read the paper. *I'll* finish the parcels. But you MUST be good and hand them out to the children tomorrow morning – yes, and hand Timmy's to him too.'

# CHAPTER TWO.

Supper-time came all too soon that night. When the bell rang to tell **the Five** that the meal was ready, they groaned.

'Have to finish afterwards,' said Dick, looking round at the mess of parcels, paper, string, ribbon and labels. 'Supper, **Timmy, supper!'**

Timmy shot downstairs at top speed, bumping heavily into Mr Kirrin, who was just coming out of his study. Timmy gave him a quick lick of apology, and ran into the dining room, putting his front feet on the table to see what was there.

'**Down,** Timmy – what manners!' said Julian. 'Hello, Uncle Quentin – done up all your parcels yet?'

His uncle grunted. Aunt Fanny laughed. 'He's going to be Father Christmas tomorrow morning and hand out all the presents,' she said. 'Don't scowl like that, Quentin dear – you **look** just like **George** when I tell her to fetch something!'

'**I do NOT scowl,**' said George, scowling immediately, of course. Everyone roared at her, and she had to smile.

'**Christmas Day tomorrow,**' said Anne happily. 'Aunt Fanny, it's lovely of you to have us all here for Christmas. We'll **never** finish **opening** our **parcels** tomorrow **morning!** I've got at least one for everybody, and so has everyone else.'

'A nice little bit of arithmetic,' said Julian. 'That means we've about forty or more presents to undo – counting in those for Joanna and Timmy.'

'What a **waste of time!**' That
remark came from **Uncle Quentin,** of course!

'It's a good thing you're not as horrible
as you pretend to be, Dad,' said George, and
grinned at him. 'You always look so fierce –
and yet I bet you've been round the shops
buying all kinds of things. Hasn't he, Mum? I
bet he's bought Timmy something, too.'

'Stop saying "I bet",' said her father. 'And don't put ideas in Timmy's head. Why on earth should I go shopping for *him*?'

**'Woof!'** said Timmy, from under the table, delighted to hear his name. He wagged his tail violently and Mr Kirrin leapt to his feet with a yell.

**'Take that dog out!** Slapping me with his tail like that! Why can't he have a short tail? I'll . . .'

'Sit down, Quentin,' said his wife.

'Timmy, come out. Sit over there. Now – let's **change the subject!'**

The four cousins looked at one another and grinned. It *was* lovely to be at Kirrin Cottage again, with dear kind Aunt Fanny, and quick-tempered Uncle Quentin. He was now beaming round at them, offering them a second helping.

'No thanks,' said Dick. 'I'm saving up for the pudding. I spotted it in the larder **– scrumptious!'**

# CHAPTER THREE

After supper they finished their parcels, and
brought them all down to the sitting room.
The tree was there, looking very cheerful,
although the candles on it were not yet lit.
It was hung with tinsel and little sparkling
ornaments, and had at the top the fairy doll
that had been on every Christmas tree since
George was little.

The parcels were put **into** a **big sack,** and this was set at the foot of the tree, ready for the morning. Timmy immediately went to **sniff** at it, from top to bottom.

'He can **smell** his **Christmas bone,**' said Anne. 'Timmy, come away. I won't have you **guessing my** present!'

Later they played games, and Timmy joined in. He was so **excited** that he began to **bark,** and Uncle Quentin stormed out of his study at once, and appeared in the sitting room.

'**George!** I've told you before I **won't** have Timmy **barking** in the house. Yes, I know it's Christmas Eve, but **I can't STAND that barking.** Why must he have such a loud one? It's enough to deafen me. I'll turn him out. He can **go** to **his kennel!'**

'Oh *no*, Dad – **not** on Christmas Eve!' said George, horrified. '**Timmy,** go and **lie down** – and **BE QUIET!**'

'He's to go out to his kennel,' said her father. 'That's my last word. **Out, Timmy, OUT!**'

So out poor Timmy had to go, his tail well down. He felt puzzled. The children had been shouting, hadn't they? It was their way of barking. Well, why couldn't *he* shout in *his* own way, which was barking?

George was cross, and Anne was almost
in tears. Poor Timmy – to be sent out to his
kennel on Christmas Eve! She went to comfort
George, and was surprised to see that she
wasn't looking upset.

'Don't worry, Anne – I'll fetch him in when we go to bed and he can sleep in our room as usual,' she said.

'You **can't** do **that!**' said Anne. 'Uncle Quentin would be *furious* if he discovered him there.'

'He won't,' said George. 'It's no good, Anne – I'm going to have Timmy with me tonight, although **I KNOW I shouldn't.** I couldn't bear not to. I'll own up to Dad tomorrow.'

So, when the household was safely in bed, George crept downstairs to fetch Timmy from his kennel. He whined softly in joy and wagged his big tail.

*'Be quiet now,'* whispered George, and took him upstairs – completely **forgetting** to **lock** the **kitchen door!**

Timmy settled down on the rug
beside her bed, very happy, and soon Anne
and George were fast asleep in their beds,
while the two boys slept soundly in their
room nearby.

# CHAPTER FOUR

**All four** were awakened by a terrific bout of **barking** from **Timmy!** He stood at the bedroom door, **scraping** at it, **trying** to **open it,** barking at the **top of his voice!** George leapt out of bed in alarm.

'What is it, Timmy? **What is it? Stop barking** – Dad'll hear you and know you're in the house and not in your kennel. **Oh DO shut up, Timmy!**'

But by this time **everyone** was wide awake, and soon the whole household was out on the landing, **alarmed.** George's father was very angry when he saw that Timmy was in the house after all.

'Why isn't he **in his kennel?** What's the matter with him? **How DARE you disobey me, George?'**

'Take him out to his kennel at once, George,' said her mother, very cross too. 'He's over-excited tonight – it was all that fun and games you had. **Take him out at once.'**

'But, Mum – he doesn't **usually** bark. Perhaps there was **a burglar** in the house,' said poor George.

'**Nonsense!**' said her father, angrily. '**No burglar** would come on **Christmas Eve.** Take the dog out to his kennel – and **don't** let me **hear another sound tonight!**'

'Go on, George, now,' said
her mother. **'Do as you're told**
and don't spoil Christmas.'

Timmy was very sad to be put into his
kennel again. He whined dismally, and George
almost made up her mind to stay outside
with him.

But his kennel wasn't big enough to take
both of them, so she gave him a hug and went
indoors with Anne, scowling in the darkness.

This time she remembered to **lock** the **door** behind her! Soon everyone was in bed again, and sound asleep.

Anne awoke a little while later and sat up in bed. She had heard something – some noise downstairs. She sat and listened. *Was* there someone in the sitting room? Then she heard a click. 'Like a **door being shut,'** she thought, and wondered if she should wake George. No – surely Timmy would bark loudly if *he* heard anything suspicious – he was only just outside, in his kennel. Perhaps he *had* **heard something** when he had barked before.

'Well, anyway, I'm **not** going downstairs by myself in the dark,' thought Anne. 'And I really daren't wake Uncle or Aunt. I must leave **Timmy** to **deal** with **whatever it is.** He can always bark or howl if **someone** is **about!'**

# CHAPTER FIVE

Timmy *had* **heard something,** and he was sitting in his kennel, ears pricked up, a little growl grumbling in his throat. He really didn't dare to bark this time. He had **heard something before,** when he had barked in George's bedroom, and awakened the whole household – and yet there had been **nobody** **downstairs** then that he could see or smell!

But **somebody *was* in the house** – someone who had crept in at the **kitchen door,** when George had left it **unlocked!**

That Somebody had **hidden** in the **coal cellar,** door fast shut, when Timmy had **barked** and **alarmed the household!**

46

Now the
Somebody was
about again, switching
on a small torch, making the
little noises that had awakened Anne.

It was **Tom,** the **bad boy of the village!** He had been out to a rowdy party, and had passed **Kirrin Cottage** on his way home. He had tiptoed to the front door, and gone to the garden door and tried both handles – no, they **were locked!** Then he had slipped round to the kitchen door, and to his surprise and delight had found it **opened** when he turned the handle.

He had crept inside and was just looking round when Timmy had begun to **bark upstairs** – and quick as a rabbit Tom had slipped into the coal cellar, and shivered there while the household came out on to the landing, angry with Timmy, who was then put into his kennel.

When all was quiet, and the dog safely in his kennel, the boy looked quietly round to see what he could take. He thought he heard a noise, and **stopped** in alarm. No, it was only the coals dropping in the grate. He felt scared, and swung his torch round and about to see what he could easily take away with him.

He saw the **sack** lying by the Christmas tree – how it **bulged** with the **parcels inside it!** Tom grinned in delight. 'Must be full of **wonderful presents!**' he thought. 'All nicely bundled up in a sack, too – couldn't be **easier** for me to carry!'

He lifted it, put
it over his shoulder, and
tiptoed out of the kitchen
door, shutting it with a little
click – the click that Anne
had heard from
upstairs!

# CHAPTER SIX

Timmy **knew** there was someone about, of course – but now he didn't **dare** to **bark**. He had been put into his kennel as a **punishment** for **barking** – if he barked again and woke Mr Kirrin, goodness knows what would happen to him!

So he kept
completely silent,
and slipped out
of his kennel,

and down the
garden path
after the boy
with the sack.

He followed him
all the way to the village,
unseen and unheard.

How he longed to growl,
how he longed to fly at this
nasty little robber-boy and
nip him sharply in the leg!

He saw the boy go through a gate and walk to **a shed** nearby. He went in,

and came out again – but this time **without the sack!**

Then he let himself into the house nearby, shut the door, and disappeared.

Timmy sat down to think. After a minute he went to the shed and slipped through the half-broken wooden door.

He **smelt** the sack at once. That bulging sack **belonged to George!** Very well – it must at once be taken back to Kirrin Cottage before the boy took out all the presents in it.

Timmy **sniffed** at the parcels inside. His **own parcel** was there – the one with the **bone** that Anne had wrapped up for him. Timmy growled.

So that **boy had DARED** to **carry away his bone!** Timmy decided to take the **whole** sack **back** to Kirrin Cottage.

But it was far too heavy for him to drag out of the shed! What was he to do?

He worked his head into the open sack neck again and pulled out **a parcel** – then **another** and **another!** Good – he would take them **one** by **one** to his **kennel** and hide them there for **Christmas morning!**

And that is exactly what dear, patient **Timmy did!** He took all those parcels **one** by **one** to his kennel, trotting **back** and **forth** so many times that he began to feel he was walking in a dream!

# CHAPTER SEVEN

It was lucky that Kirrin Cottage **wasn't far** from the boy's home, or Timmy would have been trotting to and fro **all night!**

At last the **sack was empty,**
and the last parcel safely tucked into
the back of his big kennel.

There was hardly room for Timmy to sit in it! Tired out but very happy, he put down his head on his paws, and fell sound asleep.

He was awakened next morning by a great hubbub in Kirrin Cottage!

'**Aunt Fanny! Uncle Quentin!** The **sack** of **presents is gone** – and **the kitchen door's** wide **open! Someone's stolen all** our **presents** in the night.'

'That's why **Timmy barked! He knew** there was something going on! **Oh, our beautiful presents!** What a **MEAN trick!**'

'But why didn't Tim catch the thief when he slipped out of the kitchen door with the sack? Poor Tim – he must have been too scared to do anything, after being **scolded** for **barking** before, and made to **go** to his **kennel!**'

'Christmas is **spoilt!**' said Anne, with tears in her eyes. 'No presents at all – no surprises – **no fun!**'

'**Woof!**' said Timmy, coming out of his kennel, as the four children came up the path. '**Woof!**'

'Who took our lovely presents, Timmy – and where do you think they are now?' said George, sorrowfully. 'Didn't you dare to bark?' 'Woof,' said Timmy, in an apologetic voice, and went into his kennel.

He backed out with something in his mouth – a **parcel!** He went in and fetched another – and another – **and another!**

He laid them all down in front of the astounded children, wagging his tail.

'**TIMMY!** Where did you get them? Where's the sack? Did you chase the thief, and take the **parcels one by one** out of the **sack** – and **bring them home?'**

asked George, in wonder.

# CHAPTER EIGHT

'**Woof,**' said Timmy, agreeing, and wagged his tail vigorously. He pawed at one of the parcels, and Anne gave a delighted laugh.

'That's *my* present **to *you!*'** she said. 'You *knew* it was for you, Tim – you **smelt** the **bone** inside.'

'Darling, darling Tim, how **clever you are!** You stored all our presents safely in your kennel, so that we'd have them **on Christmas morning** after all! I'll undo your parcel and you'll have *my* present **first of all!'**
**'WOOF, WOOF, WOOF!'** barked Timmy, in delight, and not even Uncle Quentin frowned at the tremendous noise.

**'Good old Timmy!** Open your parcel and then go indoors and gnaw your bone, while you watch the others open theirs.'
**Happy Christmas** to **all** the **Five** – and especially to you, Timmy-dog, especially to **you!**

If you enjoyed this Famous Five short story, there's plenty more action and adventure in the full-length Famous Five novels. Here is a list of all the titles, in the order they were first published.

1.    Five On A Treasure Island
2.    Five Go Adventuring Again
3.    Five Run Away Together
4.    Five Go to Smuggler's Top
5.    Five Go Off in a Caravan
6.    Five On Kirrin Island Again
7.    Five Go Off to Camp
8.    Five Get Into Trouble
9.    Five Fall Into Adventure
10.   Five on a Hike Together
11.   Five Have a Wonderful Time
12.   Five Go Down to the Sea
13.   Five Go to Mystery Moor
14.   Five Have Plenty of Fun
15.   Five on a Secret Trail
16.   Five Go to Billycock Hill
17.   Five Get Into a Fix
18.   Five on Finniston Farm
19.   Five Go to Demon's Rocks
20.   Five Have a Mystery to Solve
21.   Five Are Together Again